This book belongs to:

_____

GREATANGULUS TROOLLIS

GRANDMA MELOCACTA

FAMILII GRUSONIIS

CUGINIIS MIRABILIS

AUNTIE OPUNTIAE

UNCLELUS NOTOCACTULUS

TWIN COUSINUS

lacti Manor, 1912

To Pam and Martin,

who made me get on with it.

Hug Me is © Flying Eye Books 2014.

This paperback edition published in 2018. First published in 2014
by Flying Eye Books, an imprint of Nobrow Ltd. 27 Westgate Street, London E8 3RL.

Text and Illustrations © Simona Ciraolo 2014.
Simona Ciraolo has asserted her right under the Copyright, Designs and
Patents Act, 1988, to be identified as the Author and Illustrator of this Work.

2 4 6 8 10 9 7 5 3 1

Published in the US by Nobrow (US) Inc.
Printed in Poland on FSC® certified paper.

ISBN: 978-1-911171-72-0
Order from www.flyingeyebooks.com

Simona Ciraolo

Hug me

FLYING EYE BOOKS

LONDON - NEW YORK

Felipe was descended from an old and famous
family who liked to look good and
always behaved properly.

His family kept everything neat and tidy and they
believed one should never trespass into
another's personal space.

Felipe was taught
to keep still,

encouraged to be looked at

and told that one day
he'd reach a high position.

But Felipe thought his family worried
about all the wrong things.

They didn't notice that all he wanted was a hug.

Of course, he could see
his family wasn't the
touchy feely type,

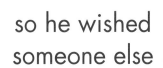

so he wished
someone else

would come and
put their arms
around him,

but no one ever did.

One day, Felipe made a new acquaintance.

He was bold, confident

and he was trouble.

But Felipe couldn't see that,

and they grew closer and closer,

until the day
disaster struck...

Felipe was blamed and made
to feel very bad.

No one in his family thought of
giving him a hug.

Clearly, he didn't belong there.

For a while Felipe hoped he would find a new family,

but wherever he went,
he wasn't welcome.

So he learned to enjoy his own company and thought
he didn't need anyone else after all.

Trespassers will be PRICKLED

UAHHHhh

During all this time
Felipe felt very lonely.

But what he didn't know was…

someone else was feeling lonely too.

The day he realized that...

Felipe knew just what to do.

BEST FRIENDS FOREVER ♡

♥ Camilla & Felipe ♥

If you liked this book, you'll love reading
these other stories by Simona Ciraolo

The Lines on Nana's Face
978-1-909263-98-7

Whatever Happened to My Sister?
978-1-909263-52-9